The cover illustration and the illustrations accompanying the text are by local artist Paul Couchman.

Paul told us: 'Producing paintings for this book of tales of the unexplained in our town has brought back memories of mysterious happenings in Leighton Buzzard. The haunted shop in Peacock Mews, the Bedford Arms to name a couple. The research for the picture of the arch gateway in the church grounds for a painting brought many ideas for ghostly tales, more so after dark. It was highly enjoyable to contribute to this publication in a creative visual way.'

To contact Paul about his work e-mail: plcouchman@yahoo.co.uk

Tales terrible and mysterious
from the Buzzard

This is Leighton Buzzard Writers' second edition of prose and poetry. Our first anthology 'Tales from the Buzzard' was produced in the summer of 2010. Two years on local writers have come together to produce a 'terrible and mysterious' collection written with the local landscape and heritage in mind. Read on to see the 'shocking' results...

Leighton Buzzard Writers

Tales terrible and mysterious from the Buzzard
A Leighton Buzzard Anthology

A collection or prose and poetry by Leighton Buzzard Writers

First published 2012

Copyright Leighton Buzzard Writers

ISBN 978-1-291-05877-2

www.lbwriters.org

Tales
terrible and mysterious
from the Buzzard

A Leighton Buzzard Anthology

A collection of prose and poetry by
Leighton Buzzard Writers

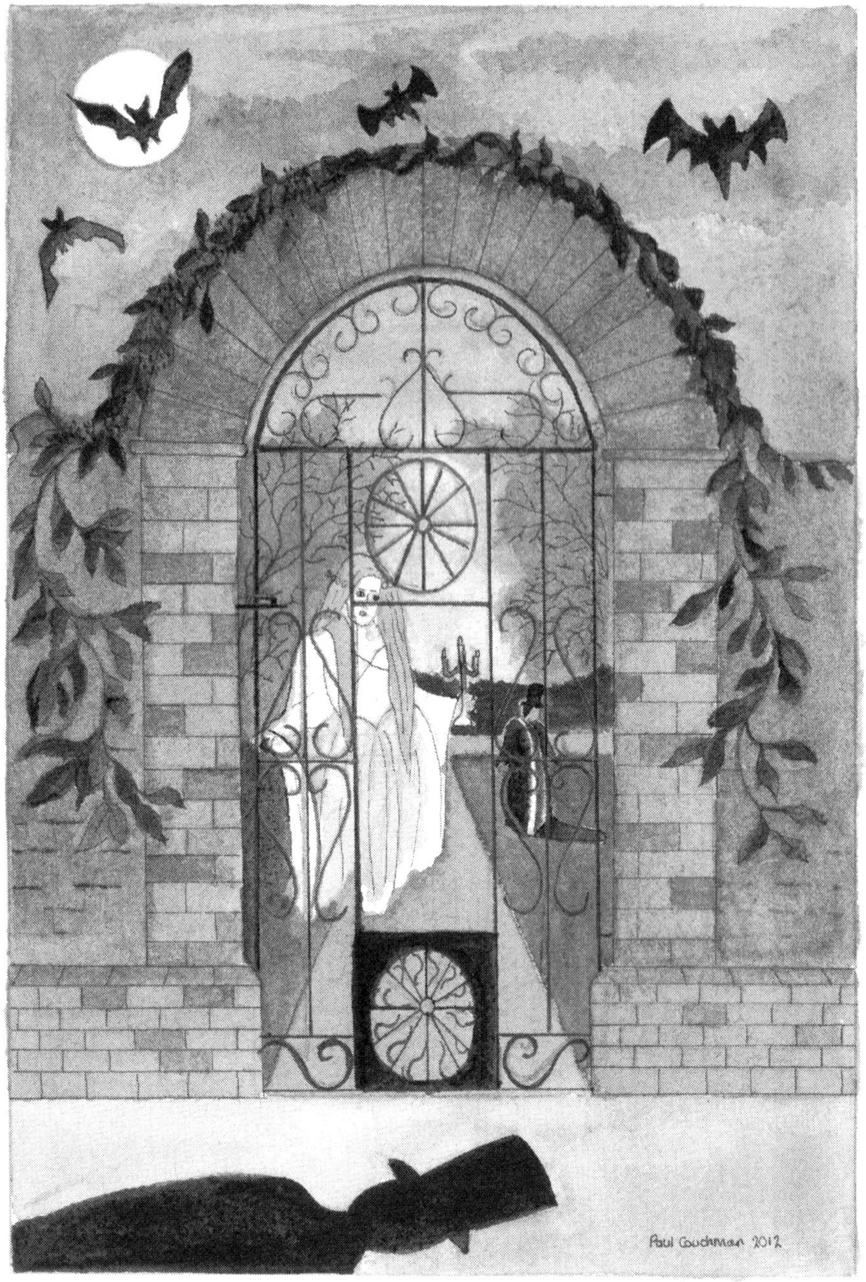
Paul Couchman 2012

Foreword

People often ask me, 'Do you believe in ghosts?' and the only answer I can give them is 'I can't say that I don't!'

A few years ago, I was asked by Chiltern Radio to lead a ghost walk around Leighton Buzzard and I found out, through my research for that walk, that the town has only two officially recorded 'ghost' incidents, an unusually low number for any town. However, whether they are recorded or not, Leighton Buzzard's history certainly contains enough circumstances and incidents that have been passed down by word of mouth over time to keep us on our toes.

The walk for Chiltern Radio began at what is now The Litten Tree public house and I began by telling a story about the building. As the group looked to the left, we saw a sign on the wall with letters that spelt out the words 'Samuel's Passage'. I'd not seen it before that evening and I've never seen it since; no marks exist on the wall to indicate its position, and no reference could be found in local records…

I've led quite a few walks since then and many people have been anxious to add to my collection of stories.

Earlier this year, I was pleased to lead the Leighton Buzzard Writers Group on a route that covered most of the sites here in Leighton Buzzard that have a story to tell.

The night was cold and damp, creating an atmosphere that sparked their imaginations. In reading this collection of stories and poems, I've been fascinated to see what has been created from the swirling mist and the legends that were related on that night.

I have very much enjoyed this collection of tales that includes the bizarre, the curious and the strange and I'm sure you will too.

Barry Grocock
Leighton Buzzard Ghost Walker
31st October 2012

Contents

The Burial Gateway: Vanessa Byham	13
The Sleeper: Vanessa Byham	15
The Bluebell Wood - 1943: Steve Gatt	21
Webbed in, in Leighton: Hannah Simpkins	27
Marika's Tale: Kathryn Holderness	31
The Dead Spot: Michael Knight	37
Presence: Terry Oakley	43
Polly's Ghost: Neil Hanley	47
The Alien Priory of Grovebury: Damien Plummer	55
All Hallows Eve: Lisa Conway	61
Time to go: Derek Hardman	67
The Statue: Phil Wilkinson	73
Neither a lender: John Hockey	81
She Didn't Know Why: Hannah Simpkins	87
The Phone Call: Karen Banfield	91
Nellie's Lock: Kevin Barham	97
Angela's Picture: Tom Tresham	103
Drifting Sands: Marilyn Downton	109
The Waiting Room: Claire Fisher	113
The Visitor Within: Hannah Simpkins	117
Sam at 'The Litten Tree': Damien Plummer	121
Relics of a Hidden World: Mike Moran	123
The Market Cross: Damien Plummer	129
A Midnight Muse: Kevin Barham	133

The Burial Gateway

By Vanessa Byham

In the low of night

In the cackling, crackling darkness

Where vine-oiled silent arms

Thrust tendrils of superstition

Twisting like mind-serpents

In the day's light, Leighton's canopied

Sun-lit arch

Becomes at night a gaping maw

The burial gateway

A passage of souls

In which horrors creep

It works upon your mind

Until

You cannot pass it without

A furtive backward glance

And hurry on

Your coat wrapped tight

Around you

The Sleeper

By Vanessa Byham

I didn't notice the storm until the first bolt of lightning struck. It must have hit something near, the sound was immense, enveloping, like an armoured embrace. The file I was working on slid across the desk and cascaded to the floor. Seconds later the rain came, crashing and battering at the windows.

The lightning struck again. Great splashing pools were forming in the road outside, lit by the sodium glare of the street light's eerie gaze. Crash and crash again. And now I felt fear. Abandoning my desk, I grabbed my coat and keys, thinking of dashing to the car. Thunder roared around the building. The lights flickered and went out. A figure blundered past outside.

Think, I told myself. Was it better to be outside or in? In, my panicking brain seemed to recall. I dashed for the stairs, and flung myself into the cellar. It was in the form of a tunnel, old and brick lined. It housed nothing and went nowhere. A few boxes of dusty files, otherwise it was the preserve of spiders and cobwebs.

The thunder rumbled and growled, it seemed to be getting worse and then one huge bolt, a Thor's hammer of a blow shook the whole building. My throat constricted. I looked around wildly, searching for I knew not what. My instinct was, get deeper, deeper underground, away from the Armageddon that was happening above. That the building might collapse around me didn't enter my head.

The torch I'd grabbed as the lights went out flickered as I made my way along the tunnel's length. Don't go out, I implored, clutching it tighter. The floor was uneven, I stumbled a couple of times. I was shivering, the air was frigid, as cold as a freezer. My breath furled in the air. The sounds receded, the silence became absolute. I tried to remember how far the tunnel went on and wasn't sure I'd ever known. Far enough to be safe, I decided, to wait out the storm.

I staggered on, hampered by the inadequate beam of the torch and the rough texture of the floor. The tunnel stretched; my mind seemed to accept that it went on further than I'd imagined. My boss had brought me down here when I started, and dismissed it with a few words. Something I'd heard though, something about rumours of a network of tunnels under the High Street, rose in my mind and a sense of excitement curled in my stomach.

The storm and my purpose for being down here receded as I delved further and further. The tunnel wound and stretched. I must be nearly halfway down the High Street, I guessed, somewhere near Wilkinsons or even the cellar of the Black Lion. Some beer, I decided, would be welcome right now. I'd promised myself a swift pint as a reward for working late, getting the files up to date.

But it wasn't the friendly outline of a beer barrel that loomed as I rounded a sharp bend, but the unexpected outline of a crouching figure. My heart began to hammer. If I was waiting out the storm – which seemed to be of biblical proportions - then it stood to reason that someone else might be too. The outline shimmered, strangely indistinct in my torch beam, then hardened as the figure rose, swung to face me, holding its arms in front of its face.

'Hi.' I dropped the torch to my side, realising I'd startled the other person, as he or she was backing away into the darkness. 'Sorry about that. I didn't expect to see anyone else down here.' I hadn't known anyone else except our offices had access to the tunnels. I hadn't long moved to Leighton; there was a lot about my new home that I didn't yet know.

Silence.

The temperature in the tunnel had perceptibly dropped. I realised my hand, the one that was clenched around the torch, felt like ice.

'I'm sorry I startled you,' I said. 'I was sheltering from the storm too, I didn't expect to see anyone. It's OK.'

It was unnerving, the two of us, standing there, the other figure stock still, seemingly frozen to the spot and me blathering away. I was an estate agent, I blathered for a living, but there was something odd about the other person, I was beginning to realise.

Throwing politeness to the wind, I raised my frozen hand and shone the torch full at the figure. Took in the white neckcloth and bulky black cloak. Sharp pointed features under a broad brimmed hat. Breeches and high boots. Breath at a standstill, I swung the torch around the dusty floor. Evidence of occupation, some blankets, a stub of candle, what looked like a Bible, a jug and a battered metallic basin...

Then the figure was gone, there was the sound of metal striking earth, heavy footsteps receding into the distance.

After a moment's stunned silence, I followed, crunching over the objects on the floor with my size tens. Dimly, I could see a set of steps going up. I reached them, poised to climb them, get outside and see where the figure had gone, when there was an almighty crack of thunder.

The torch went out, blackness enveloped and sound swirled around me, the sound of whinnying horses, shouting, bells ringing, the clash of metal on metal. Light flared, someone, many someones, were descending from the top of the stairs. Fear thickened my throat. I turned on my heel, ran, ran into the darkness, blundering and colliding with the tunnel walls in my blind flight.

I was breathing hard when I reached the entrance to our cellar. My knuckles were chapped and bleeding, my trousers torn and my coat splattered with dusty marks where I had scraped the side of the tunnel. My chest was heaving as I stretched out an arm to gather my breath. My hand touched the cold metal of a filing cabinet. It steadied me, enough to turn my head to see whatever I'd imagined had been following me.

The rain was over, the wind had dropped. The lights came back on, flooding the cellar with light, illuminating the tunnel, the boxes piled against the back wall, no more than ten feet away from where I stood.

The Bluebell Wood - 1943

By Steve Gatt

Returning from Valley Farm, Jürgen scanned the camp as the rays of the early evening sun filled the gaps between the two rows of huts. The austerity was clothed in spring warmth, an orderly and secure site for several hundred men far from home. Their guards, soldiers, were respectful and relaxed within the rules established for prisoners of war.

Jürgen had been a resident for nearly two years, earning the trust of the Commanding Officer by his hard work, honesty and consideration of others. In recognition he was given a privilege valued more than any other, the freedom to wander the valley side of the Ouzel and its dense patch of old wood.

Merke, his wife of five years, lived in Dresden with their two young daughters. Apart from one letter in the second week of his captivity, Jürgen had not received any more. He feared the worst. A strong supporter of freedom, she had spoken out against the National Socialists and as a result faced continuous harassment by their officials. Her husband's fear was obvious to all that knew him, his wife had been arrested and daughters removed.

In snow, rain and sun, Jürgen left the camp by the back gate. Immediately he was walking on a bridleway and within a few steps he was standing on a ridge overlooking the Valley. The land was undulating, falling softly to a small river, hidden from view. On the other side of the Valley, were the forests of Rushmere. It was a comforting backdrop to the flood plain of the Ouzel and the old church between the paths of the railway track and the canal. For Jürgen it evoked a sense of lost happiness in his homeland, when people were allowed to lead their own lives unfettered by others.

Often Jürgen walked through the wood following a circular route. It provided a shelter from the hostilities of the outside world. The large trees, knurled with age, had branches that spread over the path, enclosing, offering protection from the deep emptiness he felt. Drinking the stillness and quietness, Jürgen's hopes revived giving him the strength to face the unknown surrounding his family. He believed it was similar to the spirit he would find in the old church below. The birdsong the choir, the rooks the guardians.

At the top of several tall trees, where the ground suddenly fell away, was a rookery. The dark birds congregated, their nests dotted in the sky on thin branches, swaying in the wind. Often a rook would be perched next to their nest, as if a sentry looking down on the activities below. Their loud, flat calls "kaah" broke into Jürgen's meditations but he knew it was part of the wood, as was the blue carpet covering the ground. He touched its completeness and found moments of contentment.

During the day, Jürgen worked on the local farms tending the animals and assisting in the fields. Although well educated, he only spoke a few words of

English but was able to make himself understood with the locals by gestures. They respected him for his hard work and polite manner.

Jürgen was not the only one who visited the wood; the Home Guard trained in its perimeter. On this day, they had set up a machine gun post for the defence of the town and railway track from enemy troops advancing along the Stoke Road. Morale was high; at last they had a real purpose in the war effort, and a powerful weapon to back it up. A test of its capabilities was arranged for that evening when most people were eating their tea. Lieutenant Bakewell, normally the Bank Manager in the High Street, not wanting to dampen his men's spirits by sticking closely to protocol, decided a short burst would not do any harm.

Jürgen had walked slowly into the wood and stood looking up at the coming and going in the rookery when there was an explosion of noise, piercing. His body fell, near a large fallen tree, onto a bed of bluebells, red dripped from the nodding petals, with the "kaah" of the rooks giving their frightened farewell as many took flight.

Lieutenant Bakewell immediately realised their dreadful mistake and ordered all to return to their drill hall. Shock was etched across his face with his voice barely under control when he reported the fatality to the Region. The men, huddled together, heads bowed, were dismissed under strict orders not to talk to anyone. The body would be recovered in the morning, in daylight.

The night hours passed slowly for the Lieutenant; wracked with guilt and remorse, he stared through the dark trying to turn the clock back. The blackness began to fade until the grey gave way to early morning sunlight. At 8.00am a small group of men including the Lieutenant, a local Doctor, two policemen and a handful of soldiers from the Camp walked solemnly along the path towards the spot where Jürgen had fallen. The rooks were looking down, observant, making no noise, and a soldier noticed a buzzard in the sky.

The rotting tree trunk came into sight and the Lieutenant could make out the now dark crimson drops on the bark. In the bluebells was a perfect impression of a body, but no body, only a couple of handfuls of large brown feathers. As the men looked on in disbelief, the rookery suddenly burst into a hail of calls. Jürgen's body was never found.

After the War, Lieutenant Bakewell tirelessly tried to find Jürgen's family to explain the circumstances and offer his heartfelt apologies, but like many of that time they had disappeared.

The rooks still gaze down on the spot where Jürgen fell as if in eternal vigil, and, on occasion, a buzzard is seen circling above the trees as a retired Bank Manager walks, and finds peace, in the bluebell wood.

Webbed in, in Leighton

By Hannah Simpkins

Caged in, surrounded on every side

Like a blanket of meshing

Everywhere I look, every exit I attempt

There they are, wrapping around me

Four walls, windows doors, every street

All engulfed in their fine silk

Their intricate designs

Perfectly produced by nature to catch prey

Am I their prey, do they want me?

Are they setting this trap to seize me?

Unsuspecting from my ordinary world

To a world of beasts and insects

Kill or survive, that's their motto

No happy endings, no forever after

Eat and live, starve and die

Survival of the fittest so they say

Gently I wipe the silk web aside

Too much of a monster to care

Human nature drives me forward

Away from their pest like existence

Free of their miniscule grasp on me

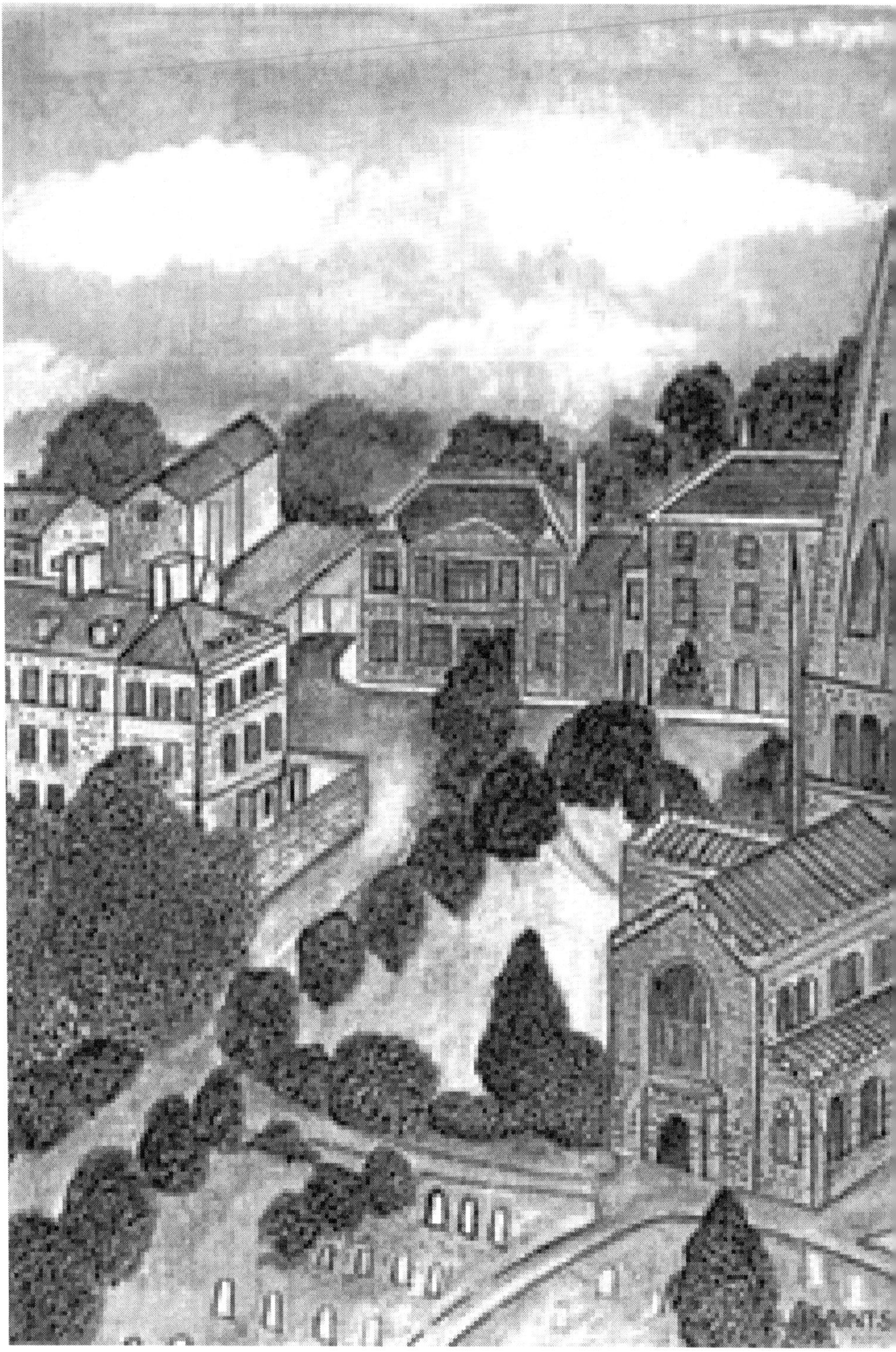

AERIAL SHOT OF ALL SAINTS' CHURCH

Marika's Tale

By Kathryn Holderness

Marika sank on to the bed and looked about her. The room was small but clean. She wished she had the energy to put the kettle on but even that was beyond her. Slowly she closed her eyes.

She awoke with a start. What was that?

'Halloo,' she heard with an accompanying rap on the door. 'Hallo there, are you in?'

Marika wanted to ignore whoever it was but perhaps that was a bad idea.

'Hallo,' she said as she opened the door. 'Yes, I am here.'

'Hey,' said the cheerful-looking young woman, 'I know you've just moved in and I thought I'd come and say hi. I'm Julie. I live downstairs. I've wondered what it was like up at the top here'. She peered round Marika taking the room in. 'Ooh, tiny, isn't it? Is it just you here? Hardly room to swing a cat, as they say? Probably used to be where the servants lived?'

'Swing a cat?' Marika looked confused. She wanted this woman to go away but was at a loss to know how.

'You're not English, are you?' Julie laughed. 'Never mind. D'you fancy coming out tonight? I'm off to the pub, meet a few mates, have a few bevvies. What's your name, by the way?'

This at least was something she understood. 'Marika'.

'Oh, that's nice. Wish my mum had thought up something better for me. I always fancied Gabriella or …'

Marika's eyes filled with tears as she thought of her mother. Julie's voice went on but all Marika could think of was her longing for those arms around her once more. And now when she had such unhappiness to bear …

'I say, are you alright? You're ever so pale and you're very thin, if you don't mind my saying so.'

'I … I've not been very well. I am ok, but not tonight. Thank you.'

Finally Marika managed to close the door. She moved to the window and gazed out. Rain was pattering lightly on the glass and through the drops she could see the twisted high branches of the towering grey tree. The church with its sodden churchyard and dark tombstones could just be made out beyond the tree. Would God ever forgive her, she wondered. But really I had no choice. Had I?

Her thoughts continued to race round her brain when a sudden movement caught her attention. There was a cat in the room, a black cat. Marika reached out to it, suddenly longing for company. Was this perhaps the cat that Julie had been talking about? But never mind, it purred happily and jumped on to her lap when she sat down. Where could she go from here? She had burned all her bridges by running away as she had – no job and no home either – and no possibility of a reference. What had Julie said? This was the room for the servants? She had been like a servant, she supposed. A modern day servant with no other home to go to. She had a little money saved up but it wouldn't last long. What then?

The room was darker now with just a little glow from a distant streetlight. Marika slept and was not aware of the cat jumping lightly to the floor and gazing intently into the mirror behind the door.

Marika awoke chilled and stiff from sleeping in the chair. Reluctantly she let the cat out aware that it must belong to someone and she had nothing she could give it. She caught a glimpse of herself as she closed the door. She smiled wryly at the thought of the trouble she used to take to look good. What had it all been for? Was she hungry? No, not really.

Her memory of the place was a little vague – somewhere she had picked because she knew no one and no one would come looking for her.

'Marika!'

What was that? Had someone called her name? It had sounded faint – not like Julie's robust tones. She hoped no one else was going to disturb her. But to call her by name? No one else knew it. She moved to the door.

The face! The face in the mirror! It wasn't hers.

Marika gasped, then looked again. No, it was her. Of course it was her. Her breathing was fast with the fright she had had. But I did see something, she whispered. It was a white face but it wasn't me. Hurriedly she opened the door. The cat miaowed and walked in. I might be going crazy, she thought, but even I don't think a cat can call my name.

Relieved, she sat down waiting for her heartbeat to slow.

The day passed slowly. Marika found it impossible to keep her thoughts at bay and wept as she remembered Alastair telling her he loved her and how then his face contorted with anger. His insistence that she must go, that any fault lay with her. His wife must never know. She should hate him. She did hate him. But oh, she loved him too.

I must go to the bathroom, she thought. I must wash my face. And as she walked to the door, the face in the mirror was not hers. But Marika's tears blurred her vision and she did not see.

Time passed. The room was cold but the cat was still there and Marika knew she was not alone. Please everyone, forgive me, she whispered. She had tried to pray for weeks but the words had refused to come. But now she felt the beginnings of peace and became aware of warmth surrounding her like a cloak which she could snuggle into.

She didn't hear Julie knocking on the door. She didn't hear her calling that she had found out some really interesting information about the history of the house and the people who had lived in it. She didn't hear Julie calling that she was going for help.

Only the cat heard.

The Dead Spot

By Michael Knight

In my garden on Vandyke Road there is a dead spot, a small area, no bigger than a man, where nothing grows, not even grass. Thinking it might once have been the location of a tree that had been uprooted and sawn up to make the creaking floorboards of my house, I spoke of it to my neighbour. He shook his head and told me a sad story that he had first heard from an old lady whose family had held our property since before the house was built.

In winter, the cows owned by the dairymen would be taken into the barns close to the dairy but, come spring, they would be let loose to wander the nearby fields close to the stream at the bottom of the rise. The daughter of one dairyman, a comely lass of 18 and betrothed to another dairyman's son, would walk among them in the spring sunshine, gathering flowers but also secretly giving milk to the feral cats of the neighbourhood.

While this act of animal charity was not wholly agreeable to her father, he did acknowledge his daughter's argument that it was those same cats that kept the barns and horse-oats free from rats, mice and voles.

One glorious April day, with her separation, churning and patting chores at the buttery finished, she was abroad, skipping through the orchard, pulling at the lower branches to make a cascade of petals which she dreamed would soon fall upon her and her man when they walked arm-in-arm from the church on their wedding day at the end of the month.

As she laughed her way down toward the stream, the cows and the place where she fed the cats, milk pail in hand, she was joined by her feline friends fully anticipating their share of the liquid bounty. She heard a noise behind her and, half turning, caught a glimpse of something dark, then became aware of the rank stench as the blow intended for the back of her head caught the side of her face, ripping into her ear and fracturing her cheekbone.

She screamed from the pain and the fear that invaded her senses, but also from the rage that welled up inside her, summoning her to swing the milk pail at her attacker, but the second blow struck her squarely under the chin, lifting her from her feet, the pail loosed from her hand falling below her as oblivion shut down her mind.

Three men, her father, her brother and her intended, each working near different parts of the orchard, heard the first scream and, recognising the voice, immediately ran in its direction.

As the men moved they heard the scream change into a shrill screeching and caterwauling. Nearing the source, each from a different direction, they became aware of a writhing mass in the grass below an apple tree. As they arrived, a dozen or more cats scattered among the trees, leaving the men to find a vagrant with his head and throat ripped apart, drowning in his own blood and vomit. Near to him lay the unfortunate girl, neck broken from falling onto the base of the milk pail that had reached the ground first and rolled directly beneath the spot where her head would land.

Bereft and overwhelmed with grief, the men looked to their beloved child, sister and betrothed, cursing the vagrant and leaving him to die where he lay.

An hour or so later the Constable and the three men returned to the spot. The Constable agreed the men's story and together they dropped the vagrant into a ditch that traversed the orchard, causing part of the side-wall of the ditch to collapse over him.

The next day, the inquest paid no heed to this impromptu disposal and dismissed the plea from the local priest to have the vagrant treated as a Christian.

'Was the besetting and killing of this girl the act of a Christian?' inquired the Coroner scathingly. 'I think not. Let the beggar lie unmarked and let the cats minister unto him.'

The dead spot is now covered by decking but each April, around the middle of the month, I notice a strange gathering of cats at the bottom of my garden. Their usual rivalry set aside, they sit on the walls and the fences, behind the flower pots and garden furniture, all seemingly watching or waiting for something on or under the decking.

At some time during the day, invariably when I am not watching, there comes the sound of a massive cat fight in the garden, which I dismiss as a typical feline falling out. Then I recall the neighbour's story.

Can cats see ghosts?

More to the point, can cats keep evil ghosts penned in hell?

I didn't think so until moving to Leighton.

Presence

By Terry Oakley

It was that feeling again,

the tingling of the hairs rising

at the back of the neck,

accompanied by the sense

of cold air falling from the ceiling,

and a chill filling the room.

The lights flickered,

the wind moaned,

the heart's beating grew louder.

The presence was here again.

Power filled the place

where they were sitting waiting.

Light flared around them

and within them.

They instinctively drew closer

as if gravity pulled them

or a force impelled them.

The silence squeezed

them tightly together

until they spoke the mystery.

Afterwards the touch of a neighbour

was both acknowledgement of awe

and relaxed relief.

The presence had been real,

the power had been realised,

the purpose was revived,

the people were renewed.

Now the inner light shone

from each and everyone

as they went out into the world.

The meeting was over

the service just beginning.

This poem was inspired by the Friends Meeting House in North Street where the Leighton Buzzard Writers meet fortnightly.

Polly's Ghost

By Neil Hanley

It all happened so fast. Polly had no chance of stopping herself; the ground just gave way. She began to slide, trying desperately to cling onto roots, branches, leaves, anything. Her hands burned along the ground. Small rocks and sharp stones stabbed at her lower back and she yelled out in pain.

She knew she couldn't fall forever. She tensed. She couldn't see what was below her feet and didn't have time to look. Then she hit something. The jarring sensation filled her whole body. She twisted and turned and then lay still in a crumpled mass. Too stunned to understand what had happened, her heart beat fast in her throat.

She looked up to see what had stopped her. Shrouded in thick ivy was a large wrought-iron gate set between two stone pillars.

It was different here.

Every time Polly inhaled she could smell damp and rot and decay. She scrambled to her feet somewhat shakily and brushed herself down. Her buckled leather sandals squelched on the spongy surface. Her arms and grey flannel shorts were streaked with dirt and her pale pink blouse, with the neat round collar, had been torn once at the side. Her neck felt stiff, but other than that she seemed okay.

She stood up and stared at the gate in front of her, not thinking or moving, hearing nothing but the faint cawing from the rooks overhead. It was a long time before she was able to think about what to do next. Until she fooled herself that she could hear voices in the distance. Maybe she wasn't that far away. She tilted her head back and yelled as loudly as she could.

'I'm here – it's Polly. Bess, are you there? Bess?'

Her voice sounded thin and shrill. The dark wood drank up her words. There was no answer. Her shouting had not made a difference. She whistled.

Nothing.

'Bess, where on earth are you?'

She cursed under her breath. If it hadn't been for that awfully silly dog, she wouldn't have fallen down that ridge. Looking beyond the gate she could see she was on the fringes of Rushmore's dense pine forest that extended up a hill. The air was filled with the aromatic tang of the decaying needles on its floor. Everything around here looked the same, whichever way she turned.

The gate was shut, but she moved further along the wall where the bricks were crumbling and noticed a large gap in the spikes protecting the top. She was good at climbing. Before her sister began to find her an embarrassment, they used to have races up the trees that grew on the common at the back of their new house in Linslade. Sometimes Susan won, but more often she did.

She dropped gingerly down onto the other side and began to follow a track that extended deeper into the woods. Every so often she'd stop to see if she could spot Bess' form through the trunks of the pines.

She looked up and saw the moon. It appeared full and high as the arms of the trees waved down at her. She felt suddenly small and very alone. Steam rose from the ground, creating an eerie mist. Fear twisted in the pit of Polly's stomach. She felt as if something was watching her.

The feeling of being watched grew stronger and stronger. It took every shred of courage for her to start walking again. It was getting late and she needed to get back soon; her mother would be going spare. A gentle breeze filtered through the trees. Polly fixed her gaze on the slope up ahead and continued onwards.

The further she walked, the darker it became and the trees didn't feel so inviting. The leaves had lost their colour and there was no birdsong, no small rustlings from some animal in the undergrowth, nothing to disturb the absolute stillness. She shivered and quickened her pace, not wanting to stay here a moment longer.

She slowed as the path disappeared and the ground again became more rugged. She paused to take a few deep steadying breaths before pushing her way through the tangled branches of a hazel thicket.

She was just beginning to feel that the woods were endless, that she might never find her way out, when she caught a flicker of movement out of the corner of her eye. She stopped dead still.

Someone – something – was creeping through the trees towards her. She jumped up and started moving forward, peeping through the trees. Was that Bess? She felt an urge to call out, but her throat tightened with fear. A strange ungainly shape lumbered across the space between two distant clumps of bracken.

Then she caught sight of the glow-worm gleaming in the glade below, beside another much larger tree. The faint light danced towards her uncertainly.

Without another thought, she scrambled behind a tree. The light danced nearer and nearer and then went out. After a while she could see the figure of a man holding a shotgun broken into his arm. There were two dogs by his side, which began to bark.

Polly went hot and cold with terror. Forcing her shaking legs to move, she ran, screaming.

Location of sighting: Leighton Buzzard, Bedfordshire

Date of sighting: 29 January 2011

Time: Approx. 2 a.m.

Witness name: Tom (Farmer)

Description:

'There have been many sightings on this old woodland site, such as dark shapes moving around, light formations and unexplained noises, including footsteps. Legend has it that one night back in 1957, when a dog hadn't returned home, the owner, a young girl, went looking for her across the old Rushmore Estate and fell down a steep ridge. Unfortunately, she died from the fall before she was found.'

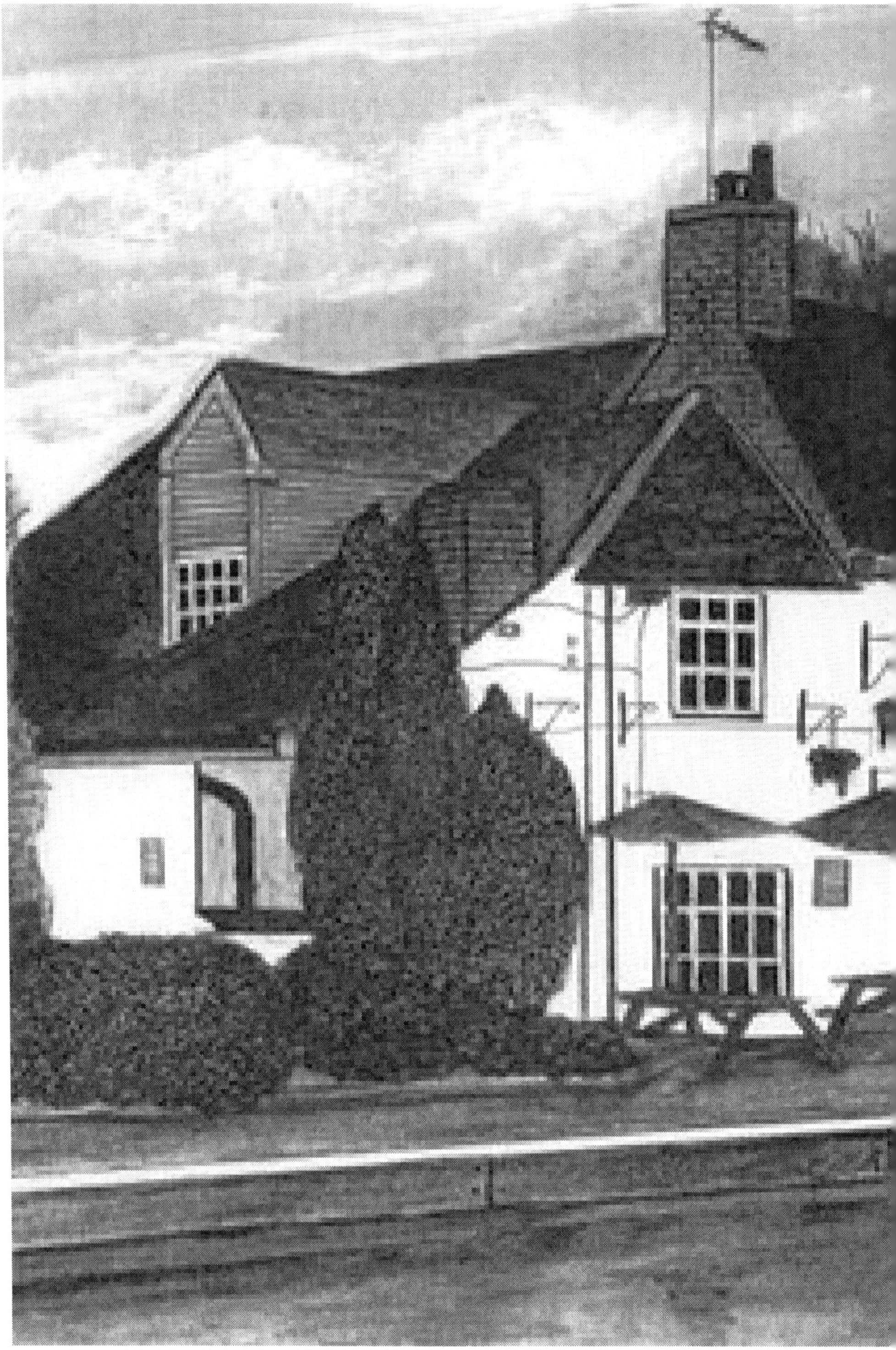

GLOBE INN AND CANAL

The Alien Priory of Grovebury

By Damien Plummer

Feminism, tragedy, the clash of Church and State, vice – once sleepy Leighton has been linked to all these through Grovebury Manor and its Alien Priory.

Despite its name, an 'alien priory' was not peopled by beings from another planet! Alien priories were religious establishments in England, such as a monastery or convent, which were under the control of another religious house outside of England, usually in France as it happened. They were settlements of foreign monks, whose main duties were collecting English rents and tithes and sending them to the mother house abroad. In Grovebury's case, its mother house was the Benedictine abbey of Fontevrault, located in the Loire Valley.

Fontevrault was unusual in that feminism ruled. This stemmed from the Rule devised by its founder, the "Blessed" Robert d'Arbrissel, a firebrand preacher known for his sympathetic view of women. The abbey was founded in 1100 and became a double monastery, with both monks and nuns on the same site. Arbrissel declared that the leader of the order should always be a woman and she was given full authority – secular and spiritual – over all the communities housed there: monks, nuns, lepers, beaten wives, and penitent prostitutes!

The link with tragedy goes back to 1164 when Henry 1 granted a £60 annuity to Fontevrault from the Royal Manor of Leighton, when his daughter-in-law, Matilda d'Anjou entered the Abbey, as Fontevrault's second Abbess. She had taken the veil after she was widowed when William, Henry's son and heir, was drowned on the infamous White Ship when it sank in the English Channel in 1120 with nearly everybody on board. Thereafter, the position attracted many rich and noble abbesses, including members of the French Bourbon royal family.

It was the 'evil' lives of the nuns of the Amesbury Abbey nuns in Wiltshire that led to their cell's dissolution there in 1177 by the order of Richard I. The cell was relocated to the Royal Manor of Leighton as a Priory under Fontevrault Abbey's direct control. It is not totally clear what the nuns had been up to, though we might speculate that their colleagues the monks may have had something to do with it! We don't know exactly how many of the nuns themselves relocated with their Cell to Grovebury, or whether those that did continued their misbehaviour (whatever it was) at Grovebury; and perhaps we shouldn't enquire too far.

Given that all the abbesses of Fontevrault were drawn from noble or even royal families, it is not surprising that some of them might meddle in political affairs. They could do this by proxy as when Grovebury's Prior refused to pay taxes to the Sheriff of Bedford in 1194 and 1247. The Abbess personally endorsed her reeve at Grovebury and 24 tenants' refusal to fight for the King in his Scottish war in 1286. The abbesses were as regal as the kings they defied!

There is always a notable exception. Edward I's daughter, Princess Mary of Woodstock, Fontevrault's Abbess from 1316 to 1324 (who was veiled as a nun at the age of 12) possessed Grovebury Manor until her death in 1332. She was known as the 'Gambling Abbess', her addiction being generously funded by her father Edward I and her brother Edward II. Mary's parents had rather generously granted her £100 per year for life (approximately £50,000 as of 2012). She also received double the usual allowance for clothing and a special entitlement to wine from the stores. Although formally abbess of Fontevrault, Mary was consigned to live at Amesbury due to Edward's fear she might fall into French hands in the event of war. That didn't stop her travelling the country and visiting court (with 24 horses, it is recorded) where she racked up considerable gambling debts. In 1305 she was given £200 to pay off the debts. This is when she was given Grovebury Priory. She also went on numerous pilgrimages, including one to Canterbury,

During the 13th century, the house at Grovebury was used as an occasional royal residence so it is more than possible that Mary might on occasion have visited her relatives there, perhaps enjoying a game or two (or three) of chance.

Could Mary have been the inspiration for Geoffrey Chaucer's Prioress in 'The Canterbury Tales'? 'Eglantine' was indeed another name for 'Mary' and we are told that the Prioress made numerous pilgrimages (as did Mary) in some state, and she seems in the Prologue to the Tale to be of noble birth. Add to that the nature of her Tale, which is vehemently anti-Semitic and is related to various blood libel stories condemning the Jews that were common at that time. As it happens, Mary's father Edward I has the dubious honour of being the monarch who banished all the Jews from England. The necklace that the Prioress wears on her neck bears the motto 'Amor vincit omnia' (love conquers all), a rather dubious maxim for a nun which perhaps takes the place of a rosary, and which certainly hints strongly at her worldliness. We know that Mary of Woodstock's notoriety continued after her death, when she was cited in a divorce case.

In 1291, Grovebury had been forcibly seized by the Crown and remained its physical property during the Hundred Years War with France. Despite papal rebuke in 1349, Edward III didn't allow the Abbess and the Abbey to "regain possession of the House of La Grava of which they have been despoiled" and, despite an attempt in 1363 to regain it for £200, it was to be forever lost.

After 1414 when Henry V dissolved all the Alien Priories, Grovebury gradually faded to become a sheep farm. The only visible clues now that Leighton ever possessed a monastic past are the ghostly outlines of the fish ponds south of Grovebury Farm that can be so easily be missed. The site of the priory itself disappeared when a quarry was dug on the site in the 1980s.

Do the shades of the naughty nuns perhaps wander the fields looking for their lost home? Might we encounter the ghost of the gambling abbess looking for a game of dice to join?

All Hallows Eve

By Lisa Conway

The ghosts of Leighton Linslade are at their happiest when darkness encircles the town and there are swathes of mist circling around on the night of Hallowe'en. They wait for the small groups of children to finish their 'Trick or Treat' visitations and then they begin to convene at the usual spot. For this is the night when they always try to find what they have lost; for some it's an object, for some a friend or relation; and for others, they have been searching for so long that they have almost forgotten what it is they're looking for.

They congregate at the site of the Holy Well, a few metres north of St Mary's Church just as pilgrims used to make their way there in the 13th century. The pilgrims were looking for miraculous cures but the ghosts are seeking an end to their searching.

First to arrive is Anne, who appears from the direction of Wing, on the old path she used in 1502. She'd been sent with offerings from Elizabeth of York, wife of Henry VII when their eldest son Prince Arthur was very ill. Following his death, Anne blamed herself for not getting to the well in time, so she continues to seek forgiveness. Then a group of Saxons appear through the mist: Oswyn was with Edward the Elder when peace was agreed with the Danes; Horsa was buried at Deadman's Slade just north of the town, but his grave was discovered by some enthusiastic Victorians; and Wilfrid lost his way on the highway known as Thiodweg in a skirmish long before the nobles of England acknowledged William of Normandy as their king.

Other ghosts and spirits come from afar for the night of 31st October, but the majority are local to the town and its more recent history.

Both Linslade and Leighton were considered to be royal manors in the time of Edward the Confessor and were recorded as wealthy royal estates in the Doomsday Book of 1086 so it's not surprising that the town remained loyal to the king during the Civil War. There were no major battles here but a great deal of pillaging went on.

One evening, a small troop of Cavaliers were on duty protecting the bridge over Clipstone Brook, then the only way into the town centre. Amongst them was a young man called Thomas. He'd arranged to meet his sweetheart and when she arrived at 7 p.m. they wandered across to the rich pastures beyond the bridge. They'd been talking together only a few minutes when Thomas could see a brigade of the Parliament's troops about half a mile away.

He persuaded his sweetheart to hide in a ditch whilst he went to warn his comrades. A few seconds after reaching them the Roundheads arrived. There was a skirmish, with all the soldiers fighting in one close and furious throng. It lasted but a few minutes. The King's troops were driven back across the stream and the Roundheads then charged away into the town. Here, they looted the houses and frightened the inhabitants before setting fire to many of the timber and thatched buildings lining the High Street. In all this upheaval, Thomas's sweetheart disappeared and so did a black stallion belonging to one of the Roundheads. Each is occasionally sighted around the town and both join the other spirits that gather on Hallowe'en. She, of course, is looking for Thomas, and the horse is looking for his master.

In 1864, a woman called Jane and her baby came to stay with the Bassett family in their house in Church Square. The baby was not very strong and, shortly after their arrival, developed a rash and a fever from which he never recovered. Jane was seen walking up and down with him in one of the windows that faces the High Street every evening until he died. She can still sometimes be seen walking in one of these upper rooms, by candlelight. She brings her candle with her to St Mary's, so that she can search every nook and cranny for her lost child.

The final guest is another woman. Her name is Louisa Bushell and usually she frequents Room 11 at the Swan Hotel. Some say Louisa committed suicide whilst others say she died of a broken heart. Whatever happened, she is obsessive about Room 11 and gets very upset if things get moved around.

Now the eight lost souls are ready to move through the swirling mist until they reach The White Horse in New Road. A notice on an outside wall advertises 'good stabling' and the black stallion is sure his master might be found here rather than near The Sun in Lake Street, where they lost each other. Next, they move down to Church Square to investigate the grounds of Leighton Middle School to search for Jane's baby. Then they float past

All Saint's church, across Parson's Field to the little path that emerges into Grovebury Road near to the point where it crosses over Clipstone Brook. Both Thomas's sweetheart, Mary, and the black stallion become frantic at this point.

Finally, they return to the High Street, where Louisa hosts their reunion at The Swan. If nothing has been found, they will drown their sorrows in Room 11, promising to meet again next year.

Anyone in the town this night with warmer blood in their veins than the ghosts might feel very unsettled if they encounter them along their journey. Perhaps you can remember being at one of the many hostelries where ghosts are said to linger; perhaps you have felt strangely cold or clammy when crossing Clipstone Brook in the autumn mists; perhaps you have already met Anne looking for the Holy Well, the Saxons in pursuit of peace, Mary looking for young Thomas, Jane searching for the baby or Louisa wanting to keep the High Street as it used to be?

….. Who's that knocking at the door?

Time to go

By Derek Hardman

It had been yet another night in the bar of 'The Swan' hotel, a situation which had become increasingly frequent of late, and which he seemed powerless to alter. In the bar he found friendship, warmth, alcohol, and above all, solace. Granted, the latter was found at the bottom of a glass, usually about the fourth, but it was there nevertheless. After the 'big event', his life had somehow lost its meaning, and he was aware that he was only marking time until his time came. The alcohol, dulling the sharpness of his mind, allowed him to forget for just a little while; after all, he was now into his seventies.

The dreaded call of the publican interrupted his thoughts.

'Time to go, gentlemen.'

He stumbled out into the High Street.

It was really cold, one of those nights where you could see to the outer limits of space. The stars cut sparkly silver holes in the black velvet of the sky, which highlighted its vastness. He gazed upwards, his thoughts a melange of melancholy, wonder, and hope. He swayed, feeling loneliness overcome him, and was then aware of just how cold it was. His ears had turned into frozen wafers, ready to crumble at a touch, and his nose had closed to the painful, biting, air. He sucked in breath through his mouth, covered now by his scarf, feeling the condensation freezing instantly on the itchy woollen fibres.

Slowly wending homewards, he realised that there was no hurry. There was no one to meet him; no welcome. Loneliness wrapped him in its shawl, as cold as the weather. Taking a short cut through the recreation park, feeling overcome by his situation, he sat down on the bench under the trees to think. His thinking, though, first of all centred on the fact that frost had already formed both on the ground and on the very bench where he sat; it was absolutely freezing. He had heard somewhere that the worst thing to do when cold was to sit down, but thought that a couple of minutes wouldn't hurt. He felt drowsy, but was pleased to find that as the drowsiness increased, so he felt warmer.

'Just close the eyes for a minute,' he decided.

He must have dozed off, for he was awoken by a whisper in his ear.

'You seem very cold dear, why don't you come with me?'

She was middle-aged, well-dressed, spoke beautifully, and had the kindest eyes he had ever seen. Although his first reaction should have been doubt, or even suspicion, he found that, instantly, he trusted her implicitly. She took his hand in hers, and led him gently away from the bench. The warmth from her hand seemed to travel up his arm and suffuse his whole body, and he accepted without question that she was caring for him.

'This must be a dream,' he thought to himself, 'I'll wake up in a minute.'

Soon she was opening the door of a flat, and taking him inside, but it was odd that she hadn't spoken another word.

'Mind you,' he thought, 'neither have I.' He was quite content to be looked after, and decided that if it were a dream, he would go along with it. It was a long time since he had felt so warm, safe and secure; cared for.

He sat down on a large, soft sofa, and she brought over a bottle of wine and two glasses. Nothing was said as she poured the wine. He sipped some, and found to his delight that it was the favourite vintage he used to have many years ago, before he was alone. He looked carefully at his companion, his eyes seemingly now focussed as never before. He still believed that he was in a dream.

She was beautiful and impeccably groomed, with just a hint of make-up to highlight the finer points of her smiling face. He found that to his delight, although nothing had yet been said, they seemed to be perfectly comfortable with each other. As she raised her glass to her lips he realised that his awareness of the situation had become heightened.

The wine in her glass was of the most wondrous hue, a deep reddish purple, with dancing diamonds of light. When she had sipped, a line of moistened wine played around her top lip, softening her ever-present smile. She wore silver earrings, which hung down and glittered in the light, creating a dazzling background to her image. They seemed to fascinate him, and hold his eyes forever to her face. He could hear lovely soft music playing, though couldn't remember when it had started, felt the comfort of the sofa, and the hint of her perfume completed the satisfaction of all his senses.

"'Please, don't let this ever end,' he thought to himself. 'I've not been as happy as this for a long, long, time.'

He closed his eyes again.

'What's it say in the autopsy report then, Sarge?' asked the young constable.

It was just a week or so after he had found the body on a bench in the recreation park. It was stiff as a board, frozen solid by all accounts. It was just another old man. Still, there was something about this one he couldn't forget. He was an old man, there was no doubt of that but, unusually, his face, relaxed in death, seemed to be smiling.

'Just the usual, my lad.' said the sergeant, "Out of the pub, then froze to death on the park bench. Officially reported as death from hypothermia. There's an odd note at the end of the report, though. It reads:

1. Unusually, the deceased, having consumed a quantity of beer, also had traces of vintage red wine in the stomach.

2. On prising open the deceased's right hand, a silver 'drop' earring was found – ownership unknown.'

The Statue

By Phil Wilkinson

I passed it every day and it looked no less forbidding whatever the weather or time. It was certainly a gruesome looking statue.

The first time I walked that route home, through Leighton's town centre, I wondered for whom the statue had been erected. It was hard to make out the writing on the dark stone plinth, but I studied it carefully and all I found were the words, 'Omnes qui scire, mori.'

Quite.

Normally I am the sort of person who passes when there are no simple answers to questions. Life is short enough without pondering over minutiae. I would rather have a beer with some friends than agonise over someone else's failure to communicate a point, or in this case, a name. Not my problem. Move on.

It had struck me one fine sunny morning that the statue seemed to be becoming grimmer despite the recent upturn in the weather. It made me wonder about its past and future. In short, it made me wonder a lot of things about it.

Today as I passed it on my way to work I wondered what the local shop owners thought about having such a depressing object stood outside their places of business. The Market Cross, by contrast, was always bright and welcoming in the sunshine. Rain merely made it uninviting with regards to sitting on its steps.

I stopped and turned back to it again to look at the words carved into the plinth upon which the brooding figure of a man was stood. His tricorne hat and attire suggested he was of the seventeenth century. Whatever century he was from, he was both ugly and fierce-looking. Why anyone thought him worthy of a statue, I really was at a loss to know.

I took my mobile phone out of my pocket and took a picture of the words. The plinth was possibly granite and this seemed to have conspired with the aging process to render the inscription invisible in the photograph I had taken. So I sent myself a text message with the words, 'Omnes qui scire, mori,' intending to ask some of my work colleagues.

Pressing the function button rewarded me a few seconds later with the sound of an incoming text message and the words for me to access later. I have just the one language and no desire to learn any others.

What with the enquiries that greeted me when I arrived at work, it was a couple of hours before I thought to ask anyone if they knew what the words meant. My expectation of a translation wasn't high. However, I didn't expect the interest and the diversity of opinion that ensued.

Various suggestions were issued regarding what the language might be. This I didn't expect. Bulgarian, Romanian, Latin, and Italian: the suggestions were all very good, but no one seemed to have a clue what it said.

Despite the numerous ideas on the language it was written in, the consensus was that it was probably Latin, or a derivative. That being so, then it probably read something like,

'All something, something dead or dying.'

That was not the greatest of help. I decided to ask those I thought had lived in Leighton Buzzard for longer than me if they had any idea who the statue celebrated or vilified.

The word 'fruitless' vied with 'hopeless' as I asked about. No one knew who the statue depicted and no one had any idea where the statue was located.

Work was beginning to take a back seat as conversations took place that I hoped would be able to throw some light on my query. My disbelief was greater and becoming louder. That so many of my colleagues, who had lived in the area for so long, didn't know of a quite prominent statue in the Market Square next to the Market Cross, appalled me.

Matt, my line manager, suggested that I could use his office computer at lunch time to look up the words on the Internet. As the computers in the rest of the office were denied access to the Internet, I jumped on his offer with glee.

A request to the IT Department for short-term access to the Internet in order to look up the meaning of a few words on a statue seemed excessive. I considered this to be especially so given that most of my colleagues seemed to be of the one view; that I had been eating too much of whatever had given me strange ideas about statues.

The rest of the morning seemed to pass a lot slower than normal. From time to time I would take my mobile phone from my pocket and read the words I had copied from the base of the statue. By the time that Matt came to me and told me his computer was now free and logged in, I must have looked at the text message dozens of times. I almost felt as if I no longer needed the record I had made. 'Omnes qui scire, mori,' almost spilled from my lips as I walked to Matt's office; imprinted on my brain as they were by now.

I felt I had allowed myself to become too wrapped up the question of the translation of the words and I endeavoured to find their meaning as quickly as possible, make a note, and determine who the man was, so as to vindicate myself to my colleagues.

Just four words to type in, but of a language that was unfamiliar to me. They felt like a random sequence of letters.

The Internet translated version came up on the screen: 'All of those who know, to die.' It seemed odd, so I simplified it in my mind and tried to make it flow more naturally. 'All those who know, die.'

The office darkened as if my eyes were slowly closing and I felt myself begin to slide to the floor. I…

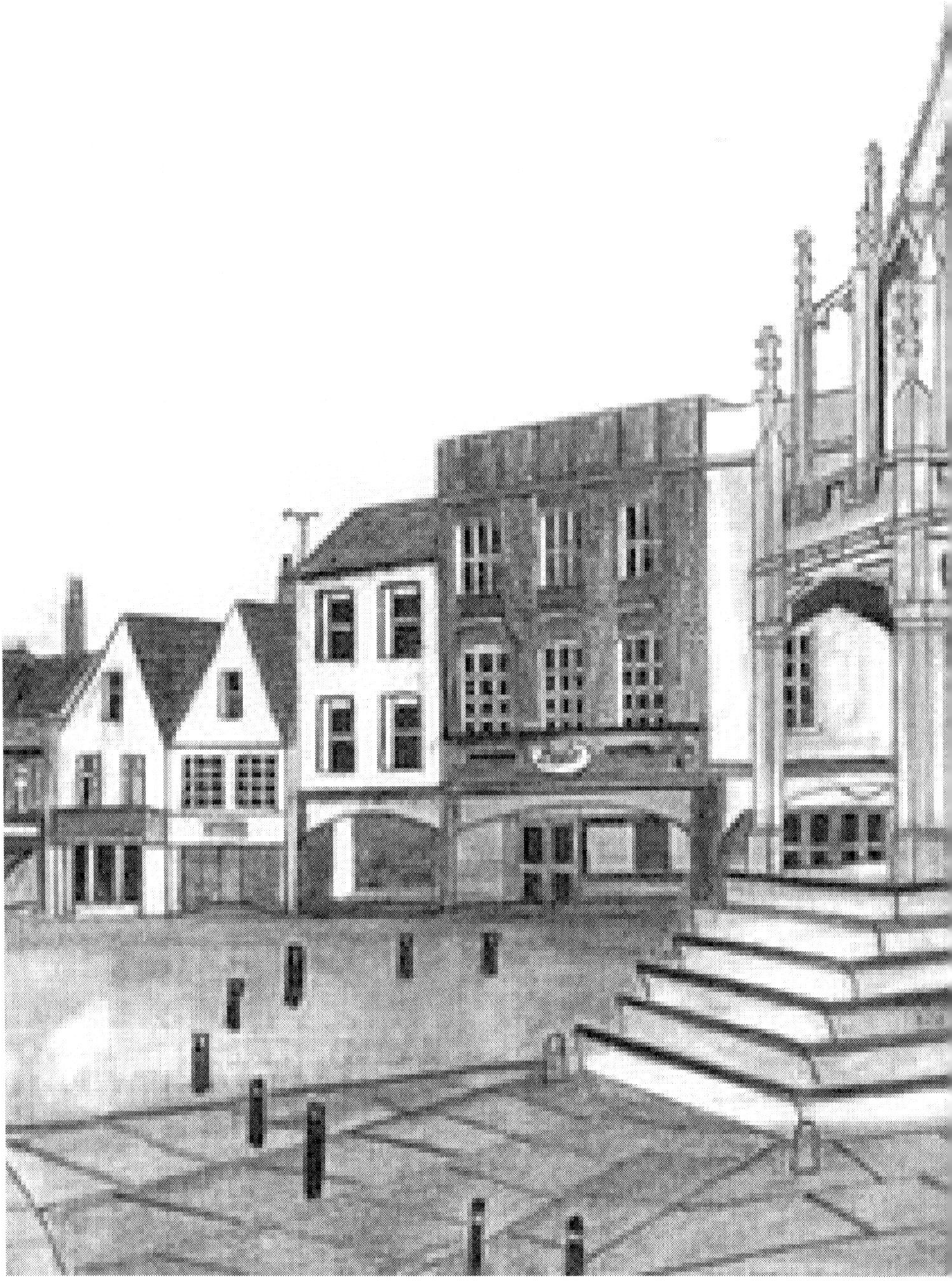

MARKET SQUARE WITH MARKET CROSS

Neither a lender...

By John Hockey

Mary sat in her high backed reading chair, gripped by the images that lay before her on the pages of the grisly novel. The drawing room was a little cool but the atmosphere seemed unnaturally chilly as she immersed herself in the story of a woman brutally murdered yet bent on ghostly revenge. Candlelight flickered on every shiny surface as reality and fiction merged into one.

On turning a page, out of the corner of her eye Mary thought she saw the curtains move. Imagination surely? But when they moved again, albeit briefly, she became unnerved and apprehensive. Her rational brain told her that if there had been a movement there was a logical cause. The wind perhaps, or a spider, or even, improbably, a mouse. But the book was working its magic and another side of her thought it might be something eerily suspicious.

Putting her book down on the mahogany pie-crust side table and rising purposefully from her chair, Mary walked towards the thick gold curtains and putting her hands in a sort of praying position, clasped the two folds of material that had moved and brought them swiftly together to crush whatever was within. As she did so, a faint, feeble cry seemed to come from the curtains and the hairs on the back of Mary's neck stood up. Gingerly she opened the folds of fabric and saw not a crushed insect or a small beast... but a bodkin. There seemed no logical explanation. How could a needle have made the movement? Perhaps there was no connection – in which case, just how had such a mundane object got stuck half way up the curtains, and what had made the eerie sigh?

Later that evening, Mary decided to do some sewing. She assembled some small shirt buttons, a needle, a silver thimble and a length of thread and set about her task. After a while, the fire which she had asked the maid to light roared into life. She felt somewhat thirsty and rising again from the chair, went for a glass of water. Upon returning to the room, Mary counted the buttons she had set aside for the shirt. One, two, three, four…five. But there had been six. And where was the thread? She began to mistrust her own memory but she was sure there had been six small buttons, and there was definitely thread – it was the thin waxed type saved especially for such tasks.

Over the coming weeks, Mary noticed other strange disappearances. There was the postage stamp that vanished when she went to answer the door on the maid's day off. Weirdest of all was the sea shell with an inside of mother of pearl that shone so brightly one might almost imagine it could be used as a mirror. One or two of the smaller, lighter items could perhaps have been blown away by a draught but not all of them, and certainly not the sea shell.

In time, Mary became less concerned about the disappearances and she started to write a sort of diary based upon what happened and who was responsible. Strangely it involved a family that mirrored her own, but in miniature. Her real mother and father wondered where on earth the girl got her imagination. Just like Beatrix Potter, they assumed it was because she was a little lonely or that she invented small friends to replace the ones that had moved away from Leighton Buzzard.

But what if, instead of a young girl's fantasy, it was all true? What if, however improbable, small humans were living in our houses and stealing items to furnish their own subterranean homes? Still not convinced? Then how would you explain what happened when the Norton family left The Cedars at the end of the High Street and the new tenants moved in? The big old house needed re-wiring and under the floorboards in the drawing room, just under where the clock had stood, the electricians found a hoard of small items. There was a needle, some waxed thread, a stamp, a button…and a shiny mother of pearl sea shell.

If, oh reader, you are still in doubt, take a look at the 1921 census for Leighton Buzzard when it becomes available. Under the entry for The Cedars and just below the details for the Norton family you will find, in faint ink, additions for a family called Clock. Head of household Pod, wife Homily and daughter Arriety. Alongside each entry, in the column marked 'Occupation' you will find written in beautiful copper plate writing the single word…'Borrower'.

This story pays due respect to Mary Norton (1903 -1992), the celebrated author of childrens' books, who lived in Leighton Buzzard for much of her childhood. Her first home in the town was The Manor House in Lake Street before she and her family moved to The Cedars, the Georgian house in Market Square at the end of the High Street. The house now consists of part of Leighton Middle School, known within the school as 'The Old House', and was reportedly the setting of her novel The Borrowers. Published in 1952, it was the first of five Borrowers' books. She began writing while working for the British Purchasing Commission in New York during the Second World War. Her first book was The Magic Bed Knob; or, How to Become a Witch in Ten Easy Lessons published in 1943, which, together with the sequel Bonfires and Broomsticks, later became the basis for the Disney film Bedknobs and Broomsticks.

She Didn't Know Why

By Hannah Simpkins

It was like they knew something before she did

The way they followed her around

It was almost a premonition she had

That something would happen, but she didn't know what

She watched the way they stalked her

The cautious steps, the leaps and bounds

She listened to the noises they made

The hoots and howls, hisses and growls

It was like they were waiting for it to begin

The way they pressed on behind

It was almost a fear she had

That something would happen, but she didn't know when

She knew if she took her eyes off the game

The way it would fall into place

She was waiting for the crowd to cheer

The knowledge that her time was near

It was like they heard it before her

The way they screamed in her ear

It was almost an epiphany she had

That something would happen, but she didn't know how

She let them slip past the action

The invisible beings moving on

She felt they knew what they were doing

The way they passed through the night

It was like they saw it before her

The way they reacted so fast

It was almost a vision she had

That something had happened, but she didn't know where

And she didn't know why

And she didn't know how

And she didn't know when it would happen in Leighton.

The Phone Call

By Karen Banfield

As I sped down the hill, it didn't occur to me what might really be happening. Ever since I moved to the town I'd been on my guard, but today I was out for the first time with my colleagues. We were sitting outside the Globe, a pretty place next to the canal, and I felt relaxed for the first time in months. I never answer my phone when it's an unknown number, but now I pressed the green button automatically.

The man's voice had a Welsh accent and he told me he worked at my vet's and they were trying to save my injured dog. I rushed to the car, hardly stopping to hear my new friends' reassurances.

I slowed down just to pass the speed camera, but hit the accelerator straight after. I found myself praying that I wouldn't lose Jimmy, not after all we'd been through together. I couldn't work out how he'd managed to escape the house when I was sure I'd locked up. I should have realised something was going on. I am so careful now, it's inconceivable I would have left the door open. But I didn't think like that, my worry for Jimmy clouded everything. The traffic slowed down for no obvious reason and I pressed my horn, shouting, 'Move, will you, move!'

Before other drivers had a chance to get angry with me, I was got going again, out of the town and down Hockliffe Road.

As I pulled into the car park, I noticed there weren't any lights on. Perhaps the vet was out in the back. I hurried towards the front door and stopped dead when I saw who was sitting on the bench, under the canopy. Gavin. Jimmy sat on his lap, happily munching on a chew bar and clearly unhurt. I went cold. At first I couldn't speak as the enormity of what had happened, dawned on me. Despite all my precautions he'd tracked me down.

Eventually I managed, 'Come here Jimmy'. But loyal as he was, his delight at the chew was overwhelming and anyway Gavin was holding him tightly.

'What do you want?' I asked.

'Well you, of course, Helena. So that we can all be together again.' He grinned and stroked the top of the Westie's head.

'How did you find me?'

'Well it wasn't easy. I'm cross with you about that, but we can discuss it later, when we're back home,' he replied, no longer grinning.

'Why did you bring Jimmy to the vet's? If you'd found out where I lived, why didn't you just wait for me there?'

I surprised myself at having the courage to ask.

'To see how loyal you are. Would you come to the aid of an animal, when you didn't come when I was in the hospital?'

'Let me have Jimmy.'

'Not yet. When we're home. If you can satisfactorily explain why you'd visit your injured dog, but not me. Even though you'd been the one to put me there.'

I felt the familiar fear rise as I recalled the last time I'd seen him. When he got home from work, the dinner I'd prepared wasn't good enough for him, again. He'd slapped me a few times and shouted at me, as I moved around the kitchen, boiling more pasta. Then he'd punched me in the stomach and caught my ribs, still healing from having been broken the previous month. Jimmy had started jumping up and barking, agitated by Gavin's raised voice. Gavin kicked him hard, knocking him across the floor. In that second, I decided to tolerate it no longer. Even if I had in some way deserved what I got, Jimmy didn't.

I picked up the scissors from the worktop and thrust them as hard as I could into Gavin's chest. He cried out as he fell down. He looked up at me and we stared at each other for the longest of moments. I thought he'd kill me. I knew then it was now or never. I scooped up a whimpering Jimmy, grabbed my handbag and ran out of that house for the last time.

And now Gavin wanted us to go home. So that he could beat me again. Or worse. But if I didn't go, what would he do to Jimmy? Gavin stood and advanced a step towards me. I knew that I wanted to survive and if I went with him, I very well might not.

'I'm sorry Jimmy' I whispered.

I sprinted across the road and up the hill, towards the shops. I soon became breathless as the road inclined. I could hear his footsteps behind me, getting closer. My heart pounded and I gasped for each breath. I ran past the florist shop straight across the junction with South Street, without even glancing to see if it was clear. Suddenly, there was a screech of tyres from behind and a dull thud. I stopped and turned around. Jimmy's head was twisted at an unnatural angle, he was definitely dead. Gavin was lying face down and cautiously I took a few steps towards him

'They came out of no-where,' the driver said, his face ashen. 'I hadn't even reached the junction and they were just there. The bloke's got a nasty gash on his neck. You put pressure on it, else he'll bleed to death the rate it's coming out. I'll ring for an ambulance.' He returned to his car.

I put my hand against Gavin's neck, pressing hard to try and save his life. Without thinking, I found myself lifting my hand up, hovering it just above, but still feeling the flow of his blood against my palm. I realised that if I just stayed like this and did nothing, he would die.

Deep down I always knew our relationship would end like this, one of us dead. I'd just always assumed it would be me.

Nellie's Lock

By Kevin Barham

Time was getting on and they were well behind Scrivener's carefully crafted schedule. It was late afternoon and soon they would have to stop and tie up for the night. Scrivener wanted to get to Leighton Buzzard before stopping. There was a pub where he and Miller wanted to while away the evening with a few pints. There would just be time for one more lock. As he steered the boat round the bend, the double lock came into view through the mist which had suddenly come down. Another boat was already nosing into the left-hand lock, so Scrivener pointed his boat at the one on the right. He drew over to the towpath so that Miller could jump off to work the gates.

Once Miller was off, Scrivener pushed on to enter the right-hand lock. He looked up to see Miller turning the windlass. As water rushed in to the lock Scrivener suddenly realised he'd never seen two locks here before. As the boat started to rise, he grabbed his Nicholson's waterways guide and looked at the map. No, there wasn't a double lock at this spot. He went to shout a word of surprise up to Miller but when he looked up Miller wasn't there... The gates swung to behind the boat.

*　*　*

Two days later, local chemist Bob Parsons was taking his border collie Murphy for his daily walk along the towpath. All the way along past Tesco, policemen were prodding the undergrowth with long sticks. Others had sniffer dogs snuffling their way along the path.

Bob was also aware of a helicopter droning somewhere overhead. Something was up.

Just past the Globe Inn, Bob saw "Captain" Bert's narrow boat tied up alongside the bank. Bert was busying himself with the stack of logs on the top of his boat, a weather-stained, rusty old craft.

Whenever Bert came down to Leighton Buzzard, Bob would pop on board and have a cup of tea with him, when the "captain" was sober that is.

'Morning Bert,' said Bob. 'What's up with all the police?'

'There's a boat gone missing,' said Bert. 'Along with both fellows on board. I told the police what I thought, but they wouldn't listen to me.'

'What do you think has happened then?' Bob said.

'There's a lot of unearthly things happen along the canals,' said Bert. 'I should know, I've been travelling 'em long enough. 'op on and I'll tell you what I know.'

Bob plonked Murphy down on the back of the boat, pulled himself aboard and followed Bert down the narrow steps into the cabin. Murphy had been on the boat before and settled down quite happily in the corner. Bert handed up a biscuit to the dog and motioned Bob to sit down. He poured two generous glasses of whisky from the bottle on the table. Handing Bob one of the glasses, he leaned across. By the look of the bottle, he'd had a couple of good shots already.

'You ever 'eard of Spring 'eeled Jack? ' said Bert. 'He's been scaring boatmen 'ere for over 'undred years. He 'ides beneath the bridges. You 'ear his footsteps and before you know it, 'e leaps clean across the canal, gets you by the throat and drags you overboard. And that's the last anyone sees of you. Nearly got me one time.'

You told the police that?' said Bob.

'No, it wasn't Jack who got 'em. Someone else,' said Bert. He took a big slug of whisky. 'Nellie's back. We're all in trouble now. Police won't find out nothing.'

Bob was uncomfortable. 'Who's Nellie?'

'She was a boatman's wife,' said Bert.

'Was?' Bob asked.

'Yeah, was,' Bert said. 'It's like this. Way back, getting on for two 'undred years ago, the Canal firm got a bit greedy and tried to get more traffic over Tring summit by building new locks alongside the old ones all the way down to Stoke 'ammond. They're all gone now. Filled in or turned into side ponds, but some of 'em you can still make out where they were. Trouble was, some of 'em were built with cheap brick. One day, Nellie and 'er 'usband were taking a load of coal down to London. They were going through one of the locks near Leighton, when it collapsed and fell in on their boat. She was up on the bank working the gates, but her 'usband and children were all killed when the boat tipped up, dog 'n' cat 'n' all. Nellie swore she'd get 'er revenge. Sure enough, a couple of years later after she died, a boat with a cargo of bricks disappeared along with the family on board. She's been coming back off and on ever since. Boats and people in the locks disappearing, nobody knows where.'

Bob, a scientist by training, wasn't impressed. 'Oh come on,' he said. 'That's all bargee superstition.'

But he could see Bert was in earnest.

'You look back in the local papers 'undred 'n' fifty years ago,' Bert went on. 'It's all there. Unsolved mysteries every few years. Police didn't know what was going on, 'adn't a clue. Boat people knew, though. O' course, the mayor and all the shops and pubs round 'ere tried to 'ush it up cos they thought it'd damage business. And don't you go calling the boatmen bargees, neither. Bargees worked the barges on the rivers. Them boats was too big to bring up the canals. People on the narrow boats was boatmen.'

Bert took another slug of whisky. 'It ain't just the boats go missin',' he said. 'Nellie's angry with everybody and everything round 'ere. If you're walking along the canal at the wrong time when she's around, she'll likely get you too. Me, I'm not staying 'ere when she's about.'

Bob laughed. 'Go easy on the Scotch, Bert.'

'You go easy yourself,' said Bert. Bob put his glass on the table and said his goodbye. He climbed up the stairs to continue walking his dog. But Murphy wasn't there... A mist was coming down.

Angela's Picture

By Tom Tresham

Angela closed the door. The house had been full of people, but had still felt empty. Dick was not there and never would be again. She supposed that funerals always left you feeling that way. Lindy, their Labrador, walked slowly across the hall and sat down at her feet looking up with sad, wistful, brown eyes.

'We'll just have to get used to being on our own now,' Angela said, petting the dog's head.

'Tea?' Mary asked, coming in from the kitchen with a tray. Mary was the kind of friend who didn't ask if she could help, but just got on with what had to be done.

'Who drew that picture of you? I don't remember seeing it before.' Mary passed a cup and pointed to the drawing of a young woman that stood on a side table. Angela was surprised to see it; she thought it was locked away in her desk.

'Actually it's not a picture of me,' said Angela.

'Not a picture of you? It's an exact likeness of how you looked when you were young.'

'It can't be me because that would be impossible.' Angela realised she would have to explain the inexplicable.

'Thirty years ago, I lived in Watford. I was in love, or rather infatuated, with a young man I knew there. One day we had a blazing row and I just wanted to get right away from him, to think. So I took a train, I didn't really care where to, but a return ticket to Leighton Buzzard was about as much as I could afford.

It was a miserable day, but I had an umbrella and I didn't really care if I got wet. When I arrived here, somehow I found myself on the towpath of the canal and just walked until I got as far as the Three Locks. I stood and looked down into the dark water in one of the empty chambers. I remember thinking that if I took one more step forward, in a few minutes all my troubles would be over. Then I heard a few notes of music. It faded and then came again from further up the canal and seemed to draw me towards it. I turned a corner and there in front of me was an old boat moored up on the opposite bank. It was still raining, but under an awning was a girl playing the flute. It was such a sad, beautiful tune, so I stood and listened. She saw me and stopped playing. I told her not to mind me, and she asked if I would like to come over and talk.

'And did you?' asked Mary.

'She threw me a rope and I pulled. A small boat that I hadn't seen before came out of the rushes and when I got in, she pulled me across. She was very beautiful, but looked rather frail. She told me her name was Lorrie and she was an artist, but when it was wet she liked to play the flute to cheer herself up. We talked together until the rain stopped and the sun came out. Lorrie asked if she could draw my picture. She was still working on it when I realised that time was getting on and I must be going. She wouldn't show me what she'd done, but she said if I came back she would finish it. I was feeling so much happier than I ever thought was possible when I had started out that morning, so I asked if she would be there next week and she said she would always be there if I needed to talk to someone.

The next Saturday was very different from the one before; fine, sunny and warm and I hurried along the towpath to where Lorrie's boat was moored, but I couldn't find it. I was sure I must have passed where it had been, but there was no sign of it. I was beginning to get very upset at not finding my new friend, when a young man came along and I asked him. He said he often walked that way but he had never seen Lorrie or her boat. We went back to the Three Locks and asked at the pub if anyone there knew anything.

'How strange,' said Mary.

'No one did, but the young man and I had lunch together and he walked me back to the station. He was really nice and asked if we could meet again. That's how Dick and I got together. Eventually we married and I never gave another thought to Lorrie and her boat until about four years ago. Dick and I went to an art exhibition at the library. All the pictures were by the same artist, Lorrain Adams. I spotted that drawing and thought it must be the woman I'd spent the day with thirty years before.

Dick bought it for me. It was only much later, when I happened to come across the exhibition catalogue again, that I found out that Lorrain Adams had committed suicide in 1939 when terminal cancer became too much for her. So it couldn't possibly have been her that I met.'

* * *

Mary came down the next morning to make the tea and get breakfast. The dog was not in her bed and Angela's coat was missing from its usual place. As she set the table, she glanced again at the picture. When she looked at it last she had seen just a face. It must have been the way the light had struck before for now she saw more detail. The sitter's body and a background of the canal were quite clear. Then she heard a dog barking in the front garden. Lindy, soaking wet and in obvious distress, scratched at the door.

* * *

Two boys cycled along the towpath above the Three Locks.

'What's that in the water?' the younger one asked, pointing to the other bank and with a tinge of fear in his voice.

His friend got off his bike and peered across at something half hidden in the rushes.

'It's alright' he said. 'It's just some old clothes. Come on or we'll be late for school.'

Drifting Sands

By Marilyn Downton

I tell not of gross hauntings, of murder most foul, or of the commoner kinds of mystery. My mysteries are elusive, I know nothing of murder, and my ghosts are an uncommon sort of ghost – they are ghosts of the far past, that is the deep beds of sand that lie beneath the environs of our small town, and ghosts of the more recent past, industrial sandpits used and disused and sandpits containing lagoons that lie on the surface.

Rocks weathered down into sand, swept up by ancient rivers and seas, carried along then released elsewhere became first desert then the sandy soils from which our town eventually raised its head. The sands beneath and around the town which, it is said, are the best sands for most purposes, originated time out of mind partly in the Pennines and partly in ancient mountains in Caledonia. However, after they dried out in their new situation, before sand-binding plants had crept across them and held them down, before sand-martins had even dreamt of risking sand-blindness and settling there, they in company with the winds must have constituted an almost perpetual sand blow: huge sand-spout pillars drawn up and along by whirlwinds and small sand-devils dancing, no place for little Tommy to play in then and not much safer for him to play in now.

Small ghosts of far-away places lay among the sand grains: 'tiny bits of gemstone, amethyst and yellow citrine,' and when men extracted sand for export some sands were carried back to where they came from in the first place.

Children always loved to play in these sandpits if they got the chance, especially in those containing lagoons. One boy 'dived into a lagoon, hit a submerged "navvy bucket", broke a few teeth and bloodied his nose.' Playing among the trucks or along the line of a light railway built early on for transporting sand were also hazardous; accidents are inevitable in such places and two boys each lost a foot by doing this. Even grown men working in sandpits have been smothered by the collapse of walls of sand exposed by excavation, so if human ghosts do exist, perhaps one or two still work at their destiny here.

Some walls of sand are things of beauty and the patterns on them can be meaningful; patterns of wavy green lines of various dimensions set in layers of sand compressed together at different angles, for instance, represent 'the cross-bedding typical of sand-waves' and ghosts of the shallow seas that covered this area at intervals in the far past.

Our town could be seen as a species of sandglass, not an hourglass for measuring time by the running-out of sand when boiling an egg, but a glass-of-aeons for the measurement by time of the running out of sand, and this drifting to and fro and round about is characteristic not only of sands but of all the phenomena cycling about the axis of the ages putting twists into their tails or doing some trick on each circuit for better or worse.

Plants, animals, people, stars and galaxies do it; even those small elements travelling up and down the Periodic Table casting bits off, or stealing bits from one another, to become something other do it. Mind does it too, and that is the greatest mystery of all. Drift, it appears, is universal, a one fits all, a mixing, an interchange, a flow, an 'as above so below,' and a search, blind or not, for the best twist for a tail or the best trick, and for the ghost of that word some say was lost at the beginning of time.

The items set in quotation marks in this piece are excerpts from Greensand Trust's 'Sands of Time project'.

The Waiting Room

By Claire Fisher

The tramp limped along the deserted station platform at Stanbridgeford. Somewhere out in the darkness, dry leaves rattled in the wind and he hugged his dirty greatcoat tighter round himself. He stopped by the waiting room. Its broken windowpanes reflected a sliver of moon.

At the back of the tiny room the tramp crouched in front of a bench. His fingers moved over the rotting wood, searching. He peered at it for a moment, and then rummaged in his old kitbag for his rusty tinderbox. It took him a few moments more to gather some bits of detritus and light a small fire. The flickering light revealed a small heart with a 'J' above and a 'P' below.

A filament of smoke rose from the fire and coiled around the tramp. A draught sighed against his cheek and he twisted round, his neck hair bristling.

'Polly?' he murmured

'Look into the fire, Joe.' The voice whispered so close to his ear that the tramp imagined it was inside his head. He jerked his hand up, but felt nothing. His eyes rested on the fire.

The flames swayed and an image formed in the heart of the fire. The waiting room appeared as it had long ago; the benches newly painted and sunlight flooding through intact panes. It was filled with people; young soldiers and their families and the tramp recalled a feeling of excitement and anticipation.

A pretty blonde girl sat on the bench with a young soldier. The young soldier was furtively scratching at the bench with a penknife and the girl giggled.

The tramp smiled and stretched his fingers towards the image, but it wavered and the flames encroached again. He threw a piece of rotting timber on the fire and it flared. Another image formed. The blonde girl was sitting on a stool; her shoulders heaved with sobs whilst next to her a baby slept in a crib.

The tramp drew a sharp breath.

'There was a baby? I didn't know.'

Around him a breeze whipped up and the fire crackled. He caught the scent of Lifebuoy soap and new wool. He looked this way and that, calling her name. The fire flared again and images streamed before his eyes: a boy dressed for school, a teenager, a doctor with a black bag. Shadows whirled around him on the waiting room walls like a magic lantern show.

'I thought you wouldn't want me. I couldn't work, I couldn't help you. I was a useless cripple.'

The tramp put his head in his hands. 'I should be dead like the rest of them.'

'You should have come back to us.' Her voice was inside his ear again.

The breeze dropped and the flames danced. When the tramp looked up, Polly stood before him. Slowly she knelt down.

'Forgive me,' he said, 'Please forgive me.'

She held out her arms and he pulled her close. Together they lay down on the waiting room floor. Joe closed his eyes and let the flames overwhelm him.

The inspiration for this story came from the deserted railway station at Stanbridgeford (now Stanbridge). The station was on the old London and North Western Railway's branch line from Leighton Buzzard to Dunstable and served the Bedfordshire villages of Stanbridge, Totternhoe, Eaton Bray and Tilsworth. Wooden passenger waiting shelters were provided on each platform. It had its heyday in the 1910s and 1920s (and was particularly busy, for example, during the First World War) but was closed in 1964. The disused timber railway buildings remained derelict until they were demolished in 1968. The track itself was removed in 1971.

The Visitor Within

By Hannah Simpkins

It's the visitor you don't invite
that should send a shiver up your spine.
They are the person in the room
when you think you are all alone.

They enter out of sight
and make your house their home.
Our homes are a temporary reprieve
from the weather and the cold.

There's plenty of them - all around this town.
They've lived in Leighton - much longer than you or I.
They like our houses - they like the designs.
They are their homes as well - they say.

They're the ghosts and the friends of those who have passed
of those who have never moved on.

But all this you'll never know.
As it's hidden at the back of your eye
In the feeling of something misplaced.

When you return from a long day out
and the curtains are slightly askance
the biscuit tin half empty
and the rug has slightly moved.

Be warned

Be afraid

Be absolutely terrified.

For those are the signs

Of the visitor within

Of the one that hides from view.

Sam at 'The Litten Tree'

By Damien Plummer

Firmly rooted in Leighton's soil

I have experienced many changes:

From Victorian townhouse to cinema,

Bingo hall to cut-price supermarket

Now, within the 'Litten Tree' function is diverse:

Coffee shop for young Mums,

Clubroom for avid knitting and crochet circles

Friends doing dinner, lunch.

Evenings, weekends infused with alcohol, music and dance

Lead to the inevitable liaisons!

Seen in passing, sensed

As a flicker, a glimmering shadow

'Almost' from the corner of the eye

Sun shimmer or phantasm?

From the opposite pavement

Raise your eyes scan

Above the 'Litten Tree' sign

Is the plaque for 'Oriel House'

The original Victorian townhouse

Friendly ghosts never leave their place of service

Where they feel most at home

Relics of a Hidden World

By Mike Moran

There is very little to remind a visitor of the existence of RAF Cheddington today, apart from a few buildings of wartime vintage which can be seen from Lukes Lane, Long Marston Road and Grubblecote. Even the concreted areas for the runways, taxiways and the apron have been torn up. A grass runway still exists, in private use for light aircraft. But this is no ordinary site of an abandoned Second World War airfield for, in the 1950s and 1960s a story with international implications unfolded here. In order to tell this extraordinary story, I have to set the scene, as follows.

In the late 1940s, the US Government was concerned that the Communists might invade Western Europe and, with the support of the UK (which provided training facilities), and other NATO governments, it set up a system of so-called 'stay behind' groups whose purpose would be to offer armed resistance against invading forces. This was known as Operation Gladio and was particularly active in Italy and West Germany, where the threat was perceived to be greatest, and where it utilised former Fascists and SS personnel. In the event, the threat never materialised but the Gladio network remained in being.

Henceforth, its role changed. It now became used to instil fear and terror into people by mounting terrorist attacks and blaming left-wing groups for them, thus leading to demands for tighter security measures. This was known as the 'strategy of tension'.

Examples of the strategy included attempts to assassinate President De Gaulle, the most serious of which occurred in 1962; the military coup in Greece in 1967; the Piazza Fontana Massacre in Milan, 1969, which killed sixteen people; the bombing of Bologna Railway Station in 1980, where eighty-five died; the Turkish Army coup of 1980; and in 1985, in the Brabant area of Belgium, a series of gun attacks on shoppers in supermarkets which left twenty-eight dead. What we must also not forget are the many efforts, often violent, to prop up the geriatric dictatorships of Spain and Portugal in the 1950s and 1960s.

In November 1990, the European Parliament passed a resolution condemning Operation Gladio as an organisation which 'has escaped all democratic controls and has been run by the secret services of the states concerned…' and 'whereas in certain Member States military secret services (or uncontrolled branches thereof) were involved in serious cases of terrorism and crime…' The resolution requested full investigations by member states into the national Gladio networks but this hasn't happened.

Thus, the scene is set for our local story.

The village of Cheddington lies a short distance to the south of Linslade. Here, in 1942, RAF Cheddington commenced operations as a satellite of the airfield at Wing, being used originally as a training base with Wellington bombers. Very soon, the US Eighth Air Force arrived with three B-24 Liberator bomber squadrons but their stay was short-lived: the American units moved to Norfolk and the RAF returned.

The Americans took over again the following year and, in 1944, B-17 Flying Fortresses, with Liberators operating alongside them, carried out secret missions at night over occupied Europe: carrying out work for the secret Special Operations Executive (SOE), such as dropping forged ration cards to cause chaos in food distribution; jamming early warning radar systems and electronic deception; and, in the latter stages of the war, dropping Safe Conduct Passes, which were later found to be held by the majority of German soldiers who surrendered.

With the war's end, the British Army took over the site and it closed in 1952. But it was not long before it was in use again as part of Operation Gladio. A network such as this needed a logistical base; so in 1956 Cheddington became the main source of weapons for Gladio. Run jointly by the CIA and MI6, and storing captured sub-machine guns, rockets, grenades and mines of Soviet origin, it was the largest secret arsenal in the whole of Western Europe.

If a coup was deemed necessary here, a political assassination there, or an act of terrorism somewhere else, Cheddington would supply the wherewithal and the weapons would not be traced back to the Americans. Instead, as the arms were of Soviet origin, left-wing groups would get the blame. It was neatly-conceived and fitted very well with the 'strategy of tension' advocated by the CIA and MI6. Cheddington even had its own CIA radio call-sign: 'X-Ray Zero Niner'.

The Great Train Robbery of 1963 brought a lot of media attention to the area and this was unwelcome to the Americans, especially when the BBC publicised the existence of the arms dump, which closed the following year. Or did it? There is mention that it was still in use in the mid-1970s, and for years after, but this is speculative.

I came in search of a mystery and stumbled upon the relics of a hidden world; a Kafkaesque tale. Unbeknown to (most, at least) residents, a small village close to Linslade was for a number of years the location of an arms centre at the service of the Cold War paranoia of Washington and London, accountable to neither judicial systems nor parliaments.

But the Cold War is over and we are safe now, aren't we?

The Market Cross

By Damien Plummer

I stand sentinel

Where the Market Square ends,

The High Street begins

Market trader probity assured

By my constant vigilance

Divine passion influences shape, form

Faith and History entwines, enriches always:

How else can Henry VI, England's puppet king

Who ruled amidst the War of the Roses bloody strife,

Rub shoulders with Hugh of Lincoln, bishop, Saint,

Whose tunic and cloak blessed All Saints?

The Madonna and Child touch John the Baptist

Who precedes his holy cousin Jesus; who facing east

Is reborn with the sun's rebirth every morning?

Old, distinctive, rather distinguished,

Preserved by itinerant preachers' use,

May 1751, saw 2 local women denounced as witch

Dragged from before me to Luton

Only by a mysterious gentleman's

Devilishly persuasive silver tongue were they saved

Town poster boy emblazoned

On postcard, tea-towel, fridge magnet, book cover

I am the Market Cross

The Market Cross's pentagonal shape is said to represent the 5 wounds Christ suffered before Crucifixion. Christ's suffering is traditionally known as The Passion.

A Midnight Muse

By Kevin Barham

Leighton Buzzard, you contain many a mystery.
Fables point to a little-known history.

Which stories here will touch you most?
Marika's tale or Polly's ghost?
A magic statue, the drifting sand?
A sleeper startled underground?
A dead spot there on Leighton's land?
Nellie's lock, the bluebell wood?
A distressing phone call that bodes no good?
The visitor within, the market cross?
Tales of terror and tales of loss.

Relics of a hidden world.
Leighton's secrets thus unfurled.

Printed in Great Britain
by Amazon